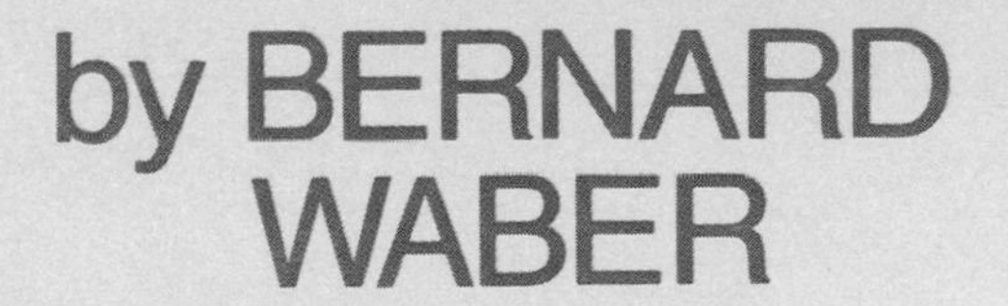

by BERNARD WABER

Bernard

Houghton Mifflin Company Boston

1982

for
Franny

Library of Congress Cataloging in Publication Data
Waber, Bernard.
Bernard.
Summary: Rather than take sides when his owners break up, a dog decides to strike out on his own and find a new home.
[1. Dogs—Fiction] I. Title.
PZ7.W113Be [E] 81-13193
ISBN 0-395-31865-3 AACR2

Printed in the United States of America
Y 10 9 8 7 6 5 4 3 2 1

Once there was a dog
named Bernard —
but that was only one
of his problems.

One day, the man and the woman
Bernard lived with had a quarrel —
a bitter quarrel.

She said,
"This is the end!
This is good-bye!"

And he said,
"Very well,
if it must be so,
then good-bye.
Come, Bernard!"

And then she said,
"But where do you think you are taking Bernard?
Bernard belongs to me, remember?"

And then he said,
"Oh . . .
but you are mistaken.
Bernard belongs to me."

And then she said,
"I saw him first.
It was at the pound. Remember?
I said, 'Oh, let's take this one,
the black and white.'"

And then he said,
"No, it was I who said that.
It was I who pointed to Bernard."

And then she said,

"You were pointing to another.
You were pointing to the one
with the wet eyes.
You were not pointing to Bernard."

And then he said,

"I raised Bernard.

I taught him all of his tricks.

Watch this!

Come, Bernard!"

“Look, Bernard! Fetch!
Bring back the glove!”

"There! Did you see?
Did you see how obediently
he brought back the glove?
I taught him to do that."

And then she said,
"Give me your paw, Bernard!
Give me your paw!"

"There! Did you see?
Did you see how beautifully
he gave me his paw?
I taught him to do that."

And then he said,
"Admit it — you never remember
to feed Bernard his vitamins."

And then she said,
"Admit it — you never think
to brush Bernard."

And then he said,

"Very well . . . perhaps there is only
one way to settle this matter.
How about if we each call to Bernard?
He will then belong to the one
he comes to first.
Agreed?" he said.

"Agreed!" she said.

They began, at once, to call Bernard.

"Here, Bernard!"

"Here, Bernard!"

"Come, Bernard!"

"Come on, boy!"

"BERNARD!"

"BERNARD!"

Bernard looked at one.
He looked at the other.
He went to neither.
"BERNARD!"
"BERNARD!"
they kept calling.

Suddenly,
without even thinking
about it,
Bernard ran away.

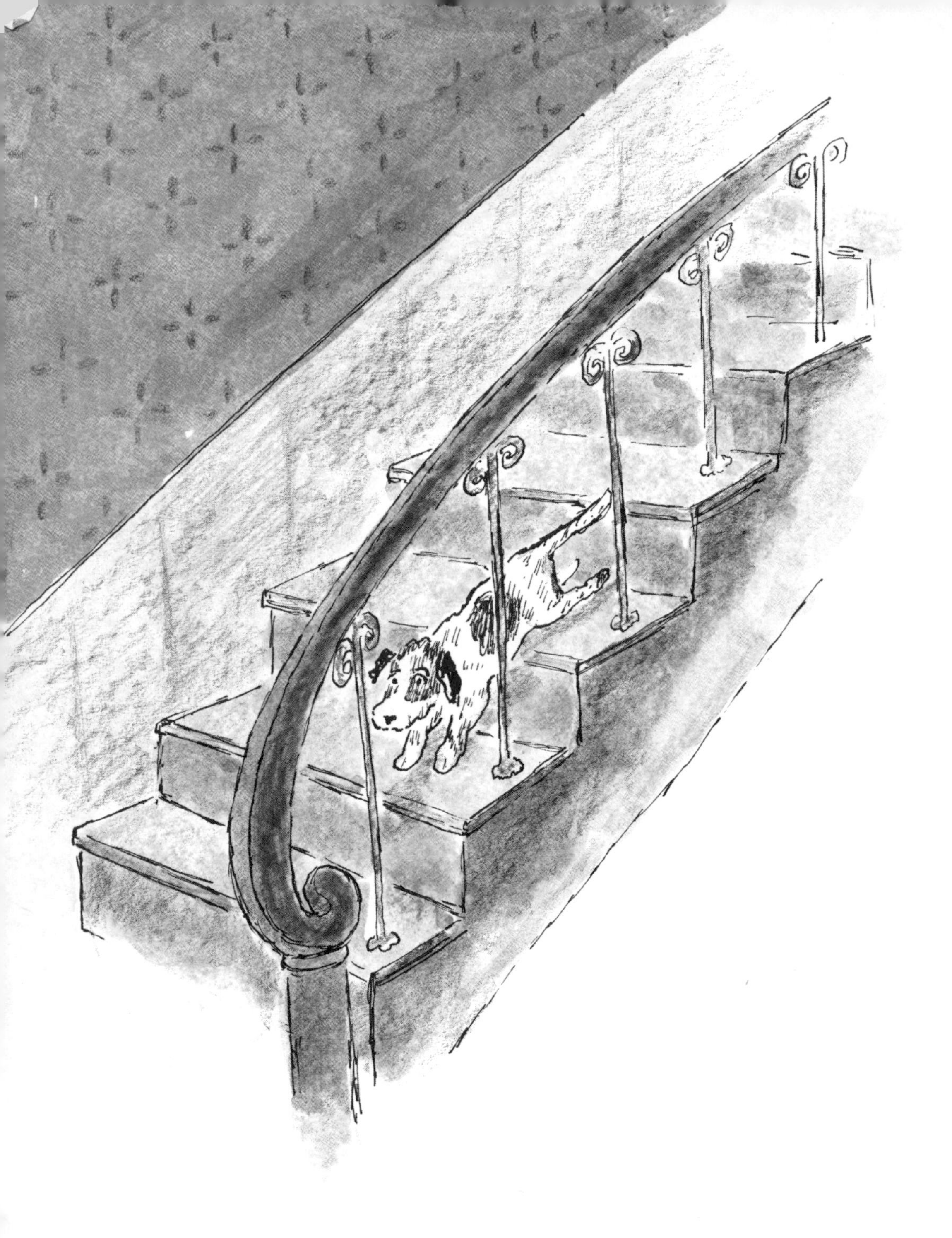

He ran and he ran . . .

until he could no longer
hear the name Bernard.

But now that he had run away,
Bernard had questions to ask himself —
important questions.
First, he asked himself,
— Isn't this most unlike a dog,
to run away —
not to be forever faithful
to those who cared for me?

And then he answered himself,

—Yes; and it bothers me. I like to
think of myself as a faithful dog.

And then he asked himself,

—But isn't it wrong, altogether, to run away?
And hadn't I better turn back?

Bernard pictured himself returning home.
He imagined the man and the woman asking,
—Well, Bernard, have you made up your mind?
Which one of us will you come to first?

And then, with sadness, he answered himself,

—Yes, it is wrong to run away.

And no,

it is not possible to go back.

I must take steps to find a new home.

— Step one, thought Bernard,
I will show I am a friendly dog.
Bernard wagged *hello* to all the people on the street.
Some stopped to pat him.
But nobody offered to take Bernard home.

— So far, not good,
thought Bernard.

Bernard saw some children.
The children were happy to see Bernard.
—Step two, thought Bernard,
I will show I am good with children.

Bernard played with the children.

He showed off all of his tricks.

Later, Bernard went with the children
and their parents to get ice cream.
Someone got ice cream for Bernard.
The ice cream had a cherry on top.
Bernard ate the ice cream,
but not the cherry.

Bernard waited to be invited home.
Suddenly, he heard the thumping of drums,
and the tooting of horns.
TAH—RUM! TAH—RUM! TAH—RUM—TUM—TUM!
Everyone began to run.
Bernard ran too.

It was a parade!
And Bernard found a front seat.
— Step three, thought Bernard,
I will show I am well behaved when
taken places.
Bernard sat quietly, enjoying the parade.

One person gave Bernard a frankfurter.
Another gave him popcorn.
Bernard ate the frankfurter,
but not the popcorn.

But when the parade was over,
nobody offered to take Bernard home.

— So far, not good,
thought Bernard.

Bernard met some truck drivers.
The truck drivers were having lunch.
They gave Bernard some salami and a pickle.
Bernard ate the salami,
but not the pickle.

Bernard saw a robber sneak onto the truck.

—Step four, thought Bernard,

I will show I am an excellent watchdog.

Bernard ran to the back of the truck.

He barked and he growled.

He snarled and he howled.

Someone called the police.
The police got the robber and took
him away.

The men climbed back in the truck
and waved good-bye.
They did not offer to take Bernard.

—So far, not good,
thought Bernard.

Bernard went to the park.
He met some people having a picnic.
The picnic people played hide-and-seek
with Bernard.

They ran
and jumped
and danced
with
Bernard.

Later, they gave
Bernard some turkey
and some coleslaw.
Bernard ate the turkey,
but not the coleslaw.
— Step five,
thought Bernard,
when they leave,
I will follow
them home.

Suddenly, the sky went dark.
And just as suddenly, there were
flashes of lightning.
The picnic people ran from the park.
Everyone ran.
Bernard ran too.

Bernard barked as he ran.
He barked at the wind, because the wind
was bending the trees.
He barked at the thunder that followed,
because it rumbled and grumbled and
sounded so much like quarreling.
He barked because everybody was
so busy running.
And nobody was paying attention to Bernard.

And now the rain came down.
It came down hard.
It splashed and it crashed.
And it rushed and it gushed.
And it plopped and it clopped.
And it burbled and it gurgled.
And it got poor Bernard
all soaking wet.
— So far, not good,
thought Bernard.

Bernard was trying hard to think of step six
when a taxi pulled up to the curb.
It splashed a giant ocean wave all over Bernard.
—Not good at all,
thought Bernard.

A man and a woman leaped out of the taxi.
She shouted,
"Look! It's Bernard! It's Bernard!
We found him! Oh, we found him at last!"

Bernard was so happy
to see the man and
the woman again.
He covered their faces
with big, wet kisses.

They immediately took Bernard home...
got him dry...
brushed his coat...

and gave him his favorite dinner.
They gave him meatballs and biscuits.
Bernard ate the meatballs,
and he ate the biscuits,
and he licked the bowl clean.

Later on, the man said,

"And now to decide how best we can share
taking care of Bernard."

And then the woman said,

"And however we decide
will be—must be—
what is best for Bernard."

"Agreed?" she said.
"Agreed," he said.

—So far, so good;
so very, very good,
thought Bernard.

And before he could think another thought,
Bernard was fast asleep.